Books should be returned or renewed by the last date above. Renew by phone **03000 41 31 31** or online *www.kent.gov.uk/libs*

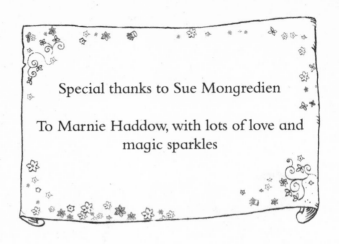

Special thanks to Sue Mongredien

To Marnie Haddow, with lots of love and
magic sparkles

ORCHARD BOOKS

First published in Great Britain in 2013 by Orchard Books
This edition published in 2017 by The Watts Publishing Group

5 7 9 10 8 6

A CIP catalogue record for this book is available from the British Library.

ISBN 978 1 40832 341 0

Printed in Great Britain by Clays Ltd, Elcograf S.p.A.

MIX
Paper from
responsible sources
FSC® C104740

The paper and board used in this book are made from wood from responsible sources

Orchard Books
An imprint of Hachette Children's Group
Part of The Watts Publishing Group Limited
Carmelite House, 50 Victoria Embankment, London EC4Y 0DZ

An Hachette UK Company
www.hachette.co.uk
www.hachettechildrens.co.uk

Phoenix Festival

ROSIE BANKS

ORCHARD

This is the Secret Kingdom

Phoenix Festival

Contents

A Mysterious Light

"I don't think I could be wearing any more clothes!" Jasmine Smith giggled to her best friends, Ellie Macdonald and Summer Hammond. "I can hardly walk!" She was dressed in a jumper, jeans and wellies, plus a thick coat, a scarf and some woolly mittens, and she had a pair of pink furry earmuffs plonked over her long dark hair.

"Same here," laughed Ellie, who had a pom-pom hat, scarf and gloves on. "I'm wearing two vests and a pair of woolly tights under my trousers. And I still feel cold!"

It was fireworks night and the three friends were out on Honeyvale Hill with their families, waiting for the display to begin. It seemed like the whole village was there too, with everyone wrapped up cosily, tucking into hot dogs and toffee apples. Summer sniffed the cold air, recognising the scent of wood smoke from the bonfire. The golden flames rose into the night, twisting and flickering. It looks almost magical, she thought.

"Anybody want a sparkler?" Ellie's dad asked, coming over with a packet.

"Yes please!" cried Ellie.

"Me too!" said Summer.

"Me three!" laughed Jasmine.

Ellie's dad handed them each a sparkler. "Remember to hold them safely, girls," he said as he carefully lit them and they burst into bright silver sparkles. "There's a bucket of water over by the hot dog stand, so once your sparkler burns out, drop it in the water to let it cool down."

Mr Macdonald went off to light another sparkler for Molly, Ellie's little sister, leaving the three friends to wave theirs, creating fizzing patterns of light in the darkness.

Summer wrote her name with hers, loving the way it sputtered and sparked. Ellie drew wild, swirling patterns in the air, like a gigantic scribble. And Jasmine made zigzaggy lines of light that seemed to hang in the dark sky for a second before fading.

"The sparkles remind me of Trixi's pixie magic," Summer said dreamily. "There's always that bright flash of light when she taps her ring to cast a spell."

"You're right," Ellie replied, smiling to herself as she thought about Trixi. She was one of their friends from the Secret Kingdom — a royal pixie who helped King Merry, the ruler there. The girls had discovered the Secret Kingdom by chance when they found a small wooden box at their school jumble sale. They hadn't known then that the box would lead them into lots of adventures in a magical land!

Once their sparklers had burned out, the girls dropped them into the bucket of water with a sizzle and a splash. Then they each got a hot dog — Jasmine added lots of fried onions to hers, Ellie squirted on a thick line of tomato ketchup and Summer kept hers plain.

They were just thinking about what to do next when a voice called out to them. "Oh, there you are, girls!" Mrs Hammond, Summer's mum, came over, holding hands with Finn and Connor, Summer's little brothers. "Summer, love, I think you've left your bedroom light on, look."

Summer and her friends turned to see where her mum was pointing. Summer's house faced Honeyvale Hill but it was hard to make out exactly where it was in the velvety darkness.

Then Summer noticed that one house had a single lit window upstairs. Oh dear – that *was* her bedroom, she could see her row of fluffy bears on the windowsill. "Sorry, Mum," she said. A frown creased her forehead. "I'm sure I turned it off though," she murmured. Jasmine and Ellie had come for tea after school that afternoon, and they'd got changed up there together. In fact, now that she thought about it, she could actually remember flicking off the light switch as they came out because they'd been plunged into darkness for a moment. Jasmine had given a pretend scream and Summer had laughed as she fumbled to find the light.

"Never mind," her mum said. "Try to remember next time. Are you all having fun?"

"Mmmm," Summer said, only half listening. She glanced back across at her lit bedroom, feeling confused…and then a shiver of excitement went through her. Could it be the light from the Magic Box that was shining up there?

"Er… Actually, we should probably go back and turn it off," she said quickly. "It's bad to waste electricity. Mrs Taylor's always saying so at school. And it'll only take a minute."

Finn stamped his foot. "I don't WANT to go back," he grumbled. "I want a hot dog!"

"Well, the three of us can go, Mum, if you give me the key," Summer suggested. "I promise I won't lose it. We'll just go straight there and come back." She could see Ellie and Jasmine giving her puzzled looks, but knew she couldn't possibly start talking about the Magic Box in front of her mum. The three friends were the only ones who knew about their magical adventures, and they wanted it to stay that way!

Mrs Hammond looked surprised too. "Don't worry," she said. "There's no need—"

"It'll only take a minute," Summer said. "Please? Anyway, I need the loo." She crossed her fingers behind her back. It wasn't strictly true about needing the loo, but she was desperate to go back to her bedroom and investigate.

If the Magic Box was calling her, Ellie and Jasmine, they needed to be there!

"Oh, all right," Mrs Hammond said as Finn and Connor began trying to drag her away to the hot dog stand. She let go of their hands for a moment to reach in her pocket and find the key. "Take my torch as well," she said, passing it to Summer. "And come straight back, okay? No messing about."

"We will, I promise," Summer replied. "Thanks, Mum. We won't be long."

As Mrs Hammond and the boys walked off, Jasmine and Ellie both looked at Summer curiously. "What was all that about?" Jasmine asked.

Summer grinned and pointed at her bedroom. "I know I turned the light off in there," she said, walking briskly across the field. "So the light we can see shining can only be from—"

"The Magic Box!" Ellie realised, breaking into a run. "Come on! What are we waiting for? Trixi needs us!"

An Exciting Invitation

Whenever there was trouble in the Secret Kingdom, Trixi used the Magic Box to send for the only people who could help – Summer, Ellie and Jasmine! All the problems in the wonderful land were caused by mean Queen Malice, King Merry's horrible sister, who was angry that the people had chosen her kindly brother as their leader instead of her.

Recently Queen Malice had unleashed a collection of nasty characters from Summer's fairytale book into the kingdom, hoping they'd cause so many problems that everyone would beg her to rule just to make them go away. But Trixi and the girls were determined not to let that happen!

"I wonder if a new fairytale baddie has appeared," Summer said anxiously as they hurried across the field. "I hope it isn't a really scary one."

"At least the ogre wasn't too horrible," Jasmine said, remembering the last baddie they'd put back in the book. He had actually turned out to be quite nice, but they'd also helped Trixi and King Merry defeat a mean giant and a wicked witch — and those two definitely hadn't been nice at all!

"Queen Malice must be getting really annoyed that we keep managing to spoil her tricks," Ellie said, feeling nervous. "I'm sure she'll be trying harder than ever to make sure her plans work out this time."

They went through the gate at the edge of the field, then crossed the quiet lane and walked the short distance to the Hammonds' house. Summer slotted the key into the lock, then pushed the front door open.

The girls kicked off their wellies and raced upstairs to Summer's bedroom. "The box *is* glowing!" Summer cried happily, rushing over to where she kept the Magic Box on her chest of drawers. "Hi, Rosa," she added, seeing her cat curled up on the bed, looking at the Magic Box in surprise. Summer's mum and stepdad, Mike, had made sure that Rosa was safely indoors so that she wouldn't be too scared by the fireworks when they started.

Ellie pulled off her hat and scarf, revealing her curly red hair, and Jasmine removed her earmuffs. Summer flicked on the main light and sat down to read the riddle that had magically appeared on the box's mirrored lid:

"Walking on water without getting wet?
You'll need to walk on me, I bet!"

"You'll need to walk on me..." Ellie repeated, thinking hard.

"What can you use to walk on water?" Summer thought out loud. "Maybe it's stepping stones?"

Jasmine stared at the Magic Box as if the answer might be hidden there. It was a six-sided wooden box decorated with carvings of prancing unicorns and

beautiful mermaids. The lid had a mirror
surrounded by six green jewels that
sparkled under the light. "Or a bridge,"
she suggested thoughtfully. "You walk
on a bridge to cross water, don't you?"

At that moment, the lid of the box
slowly lifted and a folded piece of
parchment came floating out. Summer
caught it and opened it to reveal a map
of the Secret Kingdom. "Let's see if we
can find the answer on here," she said.

The three girls leaned over the map
excitedly. The Secret Kingdom was
such a wonderful place! The parchment
sparkled with magic and didn't look
like an ordinary map at all. Instead,
looking at it was like gazing through
an enchanted window down onto the
kingdom.

"There's Magic Mountain," Ellie said, spotting its pink snow-topped peak, glittering in the sunshine. "And look, there's the ice slide down to King Merry's Winter Palace!" She smiled at the sight of two snow brownies whizzing down it.

"There's Cloud Island," Jasmine said.

"Look at the weather imps bouncing on the trampoline clouds! They're so funny."

"If we're looking for a bridge or stepping stones, we should try to find a river or stream first," Summer reasoned, then jabbed a finger at the map. "There's one!"

"And there's a bridge across it," Ellie added, spotting a huge stone bridge with a tall tower at each end. It curved over the rushing river, connecting a tiny island in the middle of the water to the crescent-shaped land.

"Firebird Bridge," Summer read out. "That must be the answer to the riddle!"

The three girls put their hands on the Magic Box. "The answer is Firebird Bridge!" they chorused.

A dazzling silver light streamed from

the box immediately, bright
with magic sparkles. The
next moment, a tiny
figure appeared in
the glittering light,
twirling on a leaf.

"Hello, Trixi,"
Jasmine said,
smiling at the
pretty little pixie.
Today Trixi
was wearing a red
dress that sparkled with glitter, and her
messy blonde hair was tucked up under
a matching hat. She almost looked like a
firework herself!

"Hello, girls!" Trixi replied, darting
around and kissing each of them on the
nose. "Nice to see you again."

"Is everything all right?" Summer blurted out. "Is King Merry okay?"

"Who's the fairytale baddie this time?" Ellie asked, biting her lip.

Trixi gave them a big smile. "Don't worry! I'm not here because of anything bad," she assured them. "King Merry's absolutely fine." She flew her leaf in an excited circle. "I came here today because I was wondering if you three would like to be our guests at the Secret Kingdom Phoenix Festival."

"Ooh, yes please," Jasmine said at once. She grinned. "I have no idea what the Phoenix Festival is, but if it's a party in the Secret Kingdom, I know I want to be there!"

"Me too," Ellie said, feeling her heart race at the thought of another trip to the

Secret Kingdom. Time stood still in the human world whenever they were in the kingdom, so they would still be back in time for the Honeyvale firework display. Perfect!

"Me three," Summer agreed with a smile. "And no baddies for a change. Even better!"

"Hurrah!" Trixi cheered, giving a little skip on her leaf. "You're going to love the fireworks. Let's go!"

Firebird Bridge

Ellie, Jasmine and Summer took one another's hands, feeling fizzy with excitement. Once they were ready, Trixi tapped her pixie ring against the Magic Box and chanted a spell:

"To Firebird Bridge over the river,
For a firework display to make us shiver!"

Jasmine beamed. She liked the sound of that! She was just about to ask Trixi about the firework display when a sparkling silver light suddenly swirled around them and the girls were swept up and away in a magic whirlwind.

A few moments later, Jasmine, Summer and Ellie were gently set down in the middle of the stone bridge they had seen on the map. The round towers at each end looked even bigger close up, and each had a pointed roof like an upside-down ice-cream cone that made them even taller. Lanterns and large white candles lined the sides of the bridge, casting twinkling reflections in the wide, tumbling river below. There was a sprinkling of stars in the velvety black sky, and the moon gleamed full and round. Groups of brownies, imps, elves and unicorns were gathered on the bridge, chatting happily. Fireflies hovered helpfully above each group, casting a golden glow so that they could see one another.

Down in the rushing water, the girls spotted mermaids splashing about playfully, their beautiful scaly tails glimmering in the moonlight. Their laughter floated up on the breeze, sounding like tinkling bells. Jasmine smiled as she saw water nymphs in the shadows – beautiful, dreamy-looking people with blue skin and wide eyes.

They seemed to be sitting on pearly
rocks, and it took her a moment to
realise that they were actually perched
on their water snails, whose curving shells
gleamed silver in the light.

"Oh, it's lovely here," Summer
exclaimed, gazing around at everything.
Her eyes shone as she saw the snails and
she smiled even wider. Summer loved all
kinds of animals, ordinary
or magical!

"It's beautiful," Ellie agreed, grinning as she noticed that their hats and earmuffs had been replaced with beautiful tiaras. Every time the girls arrived in the Secret Kingdom their tiaras magically appeared on their heads so that everyone around them would know they were Very Important Friends of the kingdom. She reached up to feel her own tiara and knew that it would be glittering as brightly as her friends' were.

"Did you say 'firework display', Trixi?" Jasmine remembered to ask. "I thought we were going to a festival."

"I did, and we are," Trixi laughed. "Oh, look, there's King Merry! Over here, Your Majesty!" she called, waving her arms above her head.

King Merry bustled over, looking very

pleased to see the
girls. "Hello,
hello, hello,"
he cried,
beaming. He
was wearing
a long purple
robe and
his crown
was balanced
lopsidedly on his
curly grey hair. "So glad
you could come to our festival. It should
be a splendid occasion."

"Thank you for inviting us, Your
Highness," Summer said politely. "We
were wondering…what exactly is the
Phoenix Festival?"

"Ahh!" the king said. "Good question.

Well, many years ago there were phoenixes living on Firebird Island – that's where this bridge goes to, you see." He pointed across to the other side of the bridge. The girls could just make out a dark island at its end, with a few scattered pinpricks of light shining in the distance.

"According to the old stories, the phoenixes could always be seen from this bridge, trailing their gorgeous flaming tails through the sky," Trixi added.

"But sadly they haven't been seen for hundreds of years – not since my great-great-grandfather, King Moody, came to power," King Merry continued.

"I think King *Merry* is a much nicer name than King *Moody*," Ellie muttered to the others.

Trixi pulled a funny face. "He wasn't the nicest ruler," she whispered to the girls. "He was said to be very moody – more like Queen Malice than King Merry."

"What happened to the phoenixes?" Summer asked. She'd read about the beautiful firebirds in stories before and would have loved to see one.

"Well, back then, there were two magical flames, one on top of each of the bridge's towers," King Merry said. "As ruler of the kingdom, King Moody should have kept the flames burning, but unfortunately he let them burn out. The phoenixes vanished, and they've never been seen since."

"Oh, no!" cried Jasmine.

King Merry looked sad. "Over the years, I've tried everything I can think of to relight those flames and bring the phoenixes back, but nothing has worked," he told them, his shoulders drooping.

"And so, every year on the night that the flames went out," Trixi went on, "we hold a special festival with fireworks to

remember the phoenixes. We still hope
that one day the magic flames will be lit
again, and the phoenixes will return to
their island." She smiled. "It's always a
great night. Our firework displays are the
most spectacular in the whole world!"

"That sounds good," grinned Ellie. "I
love our fireworks back home – but I bet
the ones here will be even better!"

King Merry nodded, looking more
cheerful. "Oh, yes," he agreed. "Prepare
to be dazzled! Our firesmiths have
been working on this year's display
for months, and they've got some very
special treats in store."

"Great," Jasmine said, nudging Ellie
and Summer with a grin as she spotted
a brownie waving a sparkler nearby.
Unlike the sparklers they'd had at home,

when the brownie wrote
her name with
the rainbow-
coloured
light, the
glittery
letters stayed
hanging in the
inky sky.

"They'll be there
all night," Trixi said
as the girls looked at the sparkles in
amazement.

"Wow," breathed Summer. "Magic
sparklers. This is going to be a brilliant
festival!"

"It certainly is," said King Merry. "I
just can't wait for it to start. I hope they
hurry up and get on with it soon!"

Trixi coughed politely. "Um... Your Majesty, I do believe you are lighting the first firework. I think the firesmiths are waiting for you!"

"Aha! So they are," King Merry said with a chuckle. "Marvellous! Well, I'd better go and do just that then. Take your places, dear girls. The show is about to begin!"

Boom!
Bang! Fizz!

King Merry marched purposefully away, with Trixi fluttering after him. "I'd better go and help!" she giggled. "I'll be back in a minute. Why don't you find a good place on the bridge to watch?" she called over her shoulder.

Ellie, Jasmine and Summer made their way to a space on the bridge and waited eagerly for the display to get under way.

"Two lots of fireworks in one night," Jasmine said with a smile. "We're so lucky!"

The girls watched as the little king headed towards the tower at the end of the bridge. Near the tower, the firesmiths – tall elves in long black aprons and sturdy boots – were hurrying about making last-minute checks on all the fireworks. Ellie saw one of them nod to King Merry to show they were ready. A second firesmith ushered the king onto a small stage, and a hush fell over the crowd. As if it had been planned, a cloud drifted across the moon, making the sky dramatically dark.

A spotlight fell on King Merry and he cleared his throat. "Good evening, dear friends," he said. "It is my great pleasure to start this year's Phoenix Festival by lighting the very first firework. And so, without further ado..."

He fumbled first in one pocket then another, a frown appearing on his face. "Ahh," he muttered, patting more pockets. "Where is it?"

"Can I help, Your Majesty?" Trixi asked, fluttering to his side.

King Merry nodded. "Yes please," he replied, still searching through his pockets. "I seem to have forgotten the... you know, the thingamajig."

"Don't worry, Your Majesty. I can help," Trixi said. "Ready when you are!"

The king smiled gratefully, then waved his hand with a flourish. Trixi tapped her pixie ring and with a whoosh the first firework shot into the sky and burst into colour.

Crack! Bang! Fizz!

Purple, red and green stars exploded above their heads and everyone gave an "Ooh!" of delight.

A blue rocket spiralled up through the darkness, looping the loop to create a glittering pattern. "Ahhhh!" sighed the crowd. Then two golden fireworks burst into sparkles that formed the shape of flying birds.

"Wow!" cried Ellie as the birds flapped their wings and flew across the sky. "That's amazing."

"Look at that one!" Jasmine added, pointing upwards. Another firework exploded with the most enormous bang, illuminating the sky with purple light. The purple sparkles joined up to form a gigantic cat that danced through the sky.

"This is so cool," Summer said, unable to tear her eyes away from the glittering sky. "Magic fireworks are so much better than the ones we have back home!"

The girls oohed and ahhed along with the crowd as a firework unicorn appeared and tossed its sparkly mane, followed by a firework that started as thousands of tiny fish, before joining together to form a diving dolphin. The dolphin firework flew down to the river and pretended to swim just above the water, making the mermaids and water nymphs jump out of the way with delighted laughs.

But just then, something strange happened. The firework unicorn suddenly pawed the air like an angry bull and galloped lower in the sky, its horn pointing forward like a jousting knight.

"Whoa!" cried a group of brownies, dodging out of the way as it landed on the bridge and galloped along.

"Hey!" shouted an elf, just managing to swerve before the firework unicorn trampled him underfoot. "Be careful!"

Up in the sky, the firework cat grew bigger and bigger until it formed the shape of a prowling tiger. With a fearsome growl, it suddenly tried to pounce on the spectators. At the same time, the firework dolphin by the river transformed into a huge glittering shark that opened its jaws as it raced towards the mermaids. With a shriek they dived beneath the surface of the water before it could reach them.

"This doesn't feel right," Summer said,

shivering. Everyone around them was
shrieking and panicking now as they
started to run across the bridge, away
from the fireworks. Over by the tower,
King Merry and Trixi were both staring
up at the sky in bewilderment.

"Something's gone wrong!" Ellie
agreed, huddling closer to her friends as
elves and brownies rushed past them.

Behind them a firework roared past
and Ellie, Summer and Jasmine ducked.
"What shall we do?" Summer asked.

"Do you think Queen Malice has
messed up the fireworks?" Jasmine
wondered. "It's just the sort of horrible
thing she would do."

"Let's ask Trixi," Ellie suggested,
thinking hard. "Maybe she knows why
this is happening."

The three of them ran across the bridge, weaving through the crowd of brownies, elves and imps who were all shouting and hurrying to get away. Summer jumped as a brownie ran past her, squealing, a firework chasing after him.

"We have to do something!" she said desperately.

At the tower, the firesmiths were running around frantically trying to put out the firework beasts with buckets of water. "This wasn't meant to happen," one wailed. "This is a disaster!"

"Stop the show!" King Merry ordered, stepping back hurriedly as the firework unicorn galloped towards him. "There is bad magic at work here. Stop this show immediately!"

"We're trying, Your Majesty," a second firesmith fretted, picking up some more water. But the bucket was knocked out of his hands by the firework tiger, who bared his teeth and looked at the firesmith hungrily. "Help!" yelled the firesmith, ducking into the shadows.

"Trixi, what's happening?" Ellie asked, running over to her.

Even cheerful Trixi looked scared. Her
face was pale and her hat had slipped
over one ear. "I don't know," she
admitted. "But the king's right – this is
the work of bad magic. Let me see if I
can trace where it's coming from. Maybe
Queen Malice is hiding up in the sky
somewhere with her Storm Sprites."

Trixi tapped her pixie ring with a
shaking finger, and chanted:

"Evil magic is in the air.
I need to know who put it there."

Bright light flashed from her ring and
thin streaks of silver scattered into the
sky. For a moment, Summer thought
Trixi's spell wasn't going to work, but
then the silver light gathered together

and flew towards a figure in the crowd, giving him a glowing outline.

Jasmine squinted to see more clearly. With so many scared people running about on the bridge, and the fireworks still sending colourful lights in every direction, it was hard to see very well but she could just make out that the figure was short with a tall, pointed hat. It definitely wasn't Queen Malice.

Then the moon slid out from behind the clouds and the whole sky brightened again. Now the friends could see that the light had surrounded an old man with thick round glasses and a pointy purple hat on his head, wearing a cloak covered in silver stars and crescent moons. "He looks like a wizard," said Ellie, then she gasped as he waved his hand over

a glowing crystal ball. Magic surged
out from the crystal ball, turning a bird
firework into a mighty hawk.

The hawk plunged down towards a
crowd of elves, its sparkling red wings
stretched wide, and the elves ran away,
squealing in terror. Then the hawk
swooped round and stared at the girls, its
red flame eyes glinting horribly.

"Run!" Ellie called as it swooped towards them, claws outstretched. The girls, Trixi and King Merry crouched down behind the tower. The hawk gave an angry squawk as it flew into the tower, scattering in a cloud of red sparkles.

"Why is he doing this?" Jasmine panted as they hid behind the tower. "Oh, no," she cried as she worked it out. "He must be another fairytale baddie, sent by Queen Malice!"

Trapped in the Tower

Just then there was a huge bang and
the sky was filled with crackling green
fireworks. The sound was so deafening
that the fleeing elves and brownies
all stopped and stared up at the sky,
watching as a flurry of green sparks
formed the shape of three long serpents
with glittering forked tongues.

The serpents began sliding through the
air at top speed, their tongues flicking
in and out. The girls peeped out from
their hiding place behind the tower and
gasped. The horrible snakes were coming
straight for them!

"Your Majesty, quick, we need to—"
urged Trixi, but before she could even
finish her sentence, the
serpents had slithered
around the tower with
a terrible hissing
sound. They
slithered right
past the girls and
wrapped their
fizzing, crackling
bodies tightly
around King Merry.

"Hahahahaha!"

Summer heard a gloating cackle and gave a startled cry to see that the wizard had appeared beside them. He raised his crystal ball and pointed a finger at the king.

"I've got you now!" he laughed. A cloud of glittering smoke appeared and the serpents tightened their hold around King Merry.

"Why, you! Get off me this instant! I command you to release me immediately!" the king blustered, trying to prise the serpents' sparkling bodies off him.

The wizard's eyes glinted coldly and his thin lips twisted in a smile. "You're my prisoner now," he gloated, rubbing his hands. "Serpents, take him up to the top of the tower!" He flung his arms out and the tower door opened with a loud creak.

"Will you get off... Aargh!" cried King Merry, squirming as he tried to get free.

The serpent fireworks were tightly coiled around him though, and he couldn't move at all. "Help!" he yelled as the serpents slithered inside the tower. "Trixi! Somebody stop this wizard!"

"I can't!" Trixi fluttered up and down on her leaf frantically, her finger on her magical pixie ring. "I can't cast a spell without hitting King Merry!"

The kindly king's voice faded away as the firework serpents dragged him inside. The wizard followed and slammed the door behind them.

Ellie, Jasmine and Summer glanced at each other fearfully, not knowing what to do. Only moments ago the festival had been a scene of great excitement and happiness, but it had quickly turned to fear and panic.

"What can we do?" Summer cried anxiously.

"Let's follow them inside," Jasmine said bravely.

"We've got to do something," Ellie agreed. "Come on, let's go."

The girls and Trixi rushed over to the door just in time to hear heavy bolts sliding across inside. They were locked out!

"Let's try some pixie magic on those bolts," Trixi said, tapping her ring.

"Unbolt this door, dear pixie ring,
I need to go and save the king!"

There was a bright flash of magic, then they heard the grating sound of the bolts sliding back.

"Well done," Ellie cheered, pushing against the door. Then she frowned. "Oh, no! It still won't open."

Jasmine tried pushing, but couldn't open it either. "There's something blocking it," she realised. "How are we going to get in now? We've got to rescue King Merry."

"And we have to get the wizard back in my fairytale book where he belongs," Summer added.

"I wonder if there's another way we can get into the tower," Ellie suggested. "There must be a window somewhere. Maybe we can climb up and scramble through it."

They stepped back from the tower so they could look, but the only window they could see was a tiny one up by the

turret roof, way out of climbing reach.
As they gazed at it, the wizard's face
suddenly appeared. He pushed open
the window and muttered a string of
enchantments, causing more fireworks to
bang and crash in the sky. A fluttering
dragonfly firework turned into a roaring
dragon, and a flower firework became a
massive fanged spider that scuttled across
the sky, making all three girls shudder.

"He's left the window open," Ellie said as the wizard vanished from sight. "We have to get up there! Trixi, do you think you could use your magic to help?"

"Let me see," Trixi said, pondering for a moment. Then she tapped her pixie ring and chanted:

"Magic powers, save the day,
And help us float up, up and away!"

The air around them flashed silver, then Summer felt her whole body become light. It was the strangest feeling! Before she knew what was happening, she, Jasmine and Ellie were floating up into the air like balloons.

"Whoa!" cried Jasmine, turning a somersault in midair. "This is so cool!"

"We're flying!" Summer laughed, her arms outstretched. "I feel like a bird."

Ellie made the mistake of looking down at the ground below and her tummy turned over. She really hated heights! "Oh, help!" she cried. "How high will your magic take us, Trixi?"

"Whoops," Trixi gasped. "I didn't tell it when to stop. Make sure you grab onto the windowsill when we reach it. Otherwise you might never come back!"

Ellie gulped. Now she was really terrified!

"Look, here's the window," Trixi said. "Quick – grab it!"

Ellie lunged for the windowsill and clung on tightly, her fingers shaking as she pulled herself through the window and drifted inside. She hurriedly pulled herself under a table to stop herself flying right up to the ceiling, with Summer right behind her.

"Phew!" Ellie gasped as she and Summer bumped against the bottom of the table.

"But where's Jasmine?" Summer

whispered frantically.

Ellie and Summer
turned round
just in time to
see Jasmine
disappearing
past the
window.

"Help!"
she squeaked.
"I can't stop!"

Summer
scrambled out
from under the table
and shot an arm through the window,
just managing to grab Jasmine by the
ankle. She hauled her clumsily inside the
room and then both girls dived under the
table with Ellie.

*"Floating magic, you can stop.
We're safely here at the tower's top!"*

whispered Trixi. The light floaty feeling
inside the girls immediately vanished and
they fell to the ground with a bump.

Peeping out from under the table, the
girls stared around the shadowy turret
room. It was large and circular, lit by
flickering candles, with thick dust on
every surface and lacy cobwebs hanging
from the ceiling. There was no furniture
except the table they were hiding under,
a large oval mirror, a dirty rug, and a
single chair. As the girls' eyes grew used
to the dim light, they realised that there
was a figure tied to it.

"King Merry!" Trixi gaped.

The kindly king was struggling to free himself. "Help!" he called out. "Oh, dearie me! Help!"

Jasmine started to scramble out from under the table, but Ellie grabbed her arm. "Listen!" she gasped.

There was a tapping sound coming from outside the door. "Footsteps!" Summer whispered.

Jasmine ducked back underneath the table just as the wizard flung open the door and walked into the room. The girls held their breath, but he didn't even glance at the table. He walked straight over to the huge oval mirror.

"Trixi!" King Merry waved as soon as the wizard's back was turned.

"Shhhhh!" Trixi flapped her arms at him from where they were hiding. The wizard looked round with a suspicious frown.

"Just ignore my brother," came a cold voice from behind the wizard. "He's not going anywhere. But you have work to do, remember."

Summer felt goosebumps all over as she recognised the voice. And sure enough, when the wizard stepped away from the mirror, she saw a familiar figure looking out from inside the glass. It was a tall woman, dressed in black, with frizzy black hair and a sour expression on her face. "Queen Malice!" Summer gasped.

Mirror Magic

Ellie, Jasmine and Summer shrank back
as low as they could under the table. The
large oval mirror was standing in front
of the stone wall and from where they
were hiding, they could only see Queen
Malice's pointy black boots. She was
tapping a foot impatiently. "Destroy the
bridge," she commanded. "Do it!"

"For you, my queen, anything," the wizard replied, bowing deeply. The queen's nasty cackling laugh echoed around the room, bouncing off the walls.

Trixi looked pale. "Oh, no!" she moaned. "Without the bridge, Firebird Island will be cut off from the rest of the kingdom. The phoenixes will never return then!"

"How can we stop him?" Ellie whispered, thinking hard. But before anyone could come up with a plan, Summer spotted the wizard striding across the room towards them.

"Shh," she warned. The girls fell silent, terrified that he might have heard them. Thankfully, the wizard seemed so distracted by his wicked plans that he hadn't noticed a thing. The girls huddled together as he leaned out of the window and snapped his fingers. By peeping round the table leg, Jasmine could see the firework unicorn gallop through the sky to the window. Then the wizard clambered through and onto its back.

"Down to the bridge!" the girls heard him yell as the unicorn rode away into the night.

Ellie, Summer and Jasmine breathed a sigh of relief. But just as they were crawling out from underneath the table, a spell exploded against the window and the room suddenly grew dark.

"He's sealed up the window with bricks," Summer whispered in alarm. "We're trapped!"

Jasmine glanced at the mirror, which looked dark and empty. At least Queen

Malice had gone. She ran to the window, hoping that she might be able to pull the bricks out before the magic locked them in for good. But it was no use – the bricks were tightly packed into the window and didn't move.

"Oh, so you sneaked in, did you?" came a snarl from behind her.

Jasmine gasped and turned to see their enemy back in the mirror again. Malice's gaze flicked to the table, and before Jasmine could move, the wicked queen pointed her staff at where Summer and Ellie were hidden.

"No!" Jasmine yelled, but it was too late. A lightning bolt shot out of the glass, flipping the table over to reveal Summer and Ellie crouching there, with Trixi hovering nearby on her leaf.

"How sweet," cackled Queen Malice. "Were you trying to save my pathetic brother again? I really don't think he's worth the effort, you know." She tipped her head back and gave a screechy laugh, then stamped her foot on the floor. "You're out of luck this time, girls," she said, her voice dripping with ice. "You're stuck here for good. For ever, I hope. Ha!"

"Sister, you've gone too far!" said King Merry, his face red with anger as he struggled on the chair.

"Please don't let the wizard destroy the bridge," Trixi pleaded desperately. "Please!"

Malice looked first at her brother, then at the royal pixie with great scorn. "Too late," she sneered. "The wizard will be blowing it up any second now. You can all stay here – until the tower tumbles down, that is." She gave a cackling laugh, then paused thoughtfully. "I've had a lot of trouble with you girls lately," she added. "Perhaps I'd better make sure you won't try and escape."

She flicked her fingers above her head. The surface of the mirror clouded over again and she disappeared from sight, but three smaller figures appeared. As the image in the glass cleared, the girls could see their grey bodies, pointy fingers and bat-like wings. "Oh, no," cried Summer. "Storm Sprites!"

The Storm Sprites were Queen Malice's helpers, who travelled on mini thunderclouds. One burst through the mirror in a little shower of rain, grinning nastily, while another scrambled out behind him.

"Quick!" shouted Jasmine, grabbing the rug and throwing it over the Storm Sprites' heads.

Ellie and Summer rushed to untie King Merry, their fingers fumbling over the knotted rope.

"Hey! It's all gone dark!" cried the Storm Sprites, thrashing around under the rug.

"Hurry," called Ellie as soon as King Merry was free. Leaving the Storm Sprites still stuck under the rug, she and her friends dashed through the door and rushed out into the hall. A spiral staircase led down to the ground.

"But the door's blocked, remember!" Summer realised with alarm. "We still won't be able to get out."

"Well, we can't stay here," Ellie said,

glancing back at the struggling Storm Sprites. "If the wizard destroys the bridge, the tower will fall down too!"

"We won't let that happen!" Jasmine said determinedly as she took off down the stone steps.

"Are you all right, Your Majesty? Are you hurt?" Trixi asked anxiously as they followed Jasmine.

"No, no... Don't worry about me," the king panted. "We have...to stop...that wizard!"

"We will," Summer replied, running down the curling steps as fast as she could. "Whatever happens, we can't let him destroy the bridge!"

The Last Firework

King Merry, Trixi and the girls ran down
the spiral steps so fast they felt dizzy.
Suddenly Jasmine stopped and the others
skidded to a halt behind her. The door
to the tower was blocked by a huge suit
of armour. "No wonder we couldn't get
in!" Jasmine breathed.

As the girls began to try and push the
armour out of the way, there was the
sound of pounding feet on the staircase.

The Storm Sprites were coming!

"I can't move it," Jasmine panted. "It's so heavy!"

"Hurry, I can hear the Storm Sprites!" Summer pushed even harder. Outside she could hear fireworks banging and cracking overhead. Or was that the sound of the bridge being blown up?

King Merry started pushing the armour so hard that his face turned bright red. "We. Have. To. Save. The. Bridge!" he puffed.

"It's working!" Ellie cried as the armour started

to move. All the girls gave a huge heave and suddenly the armour clattered into pieces on the floor. Then King Merry shoved open the door, and they all tumbled out into the cool night air.

The wizard was at one end of the bridge, his arms raised above his head as he directed the fireworks through the sky. "Come, my firework beasts," he called. "Serve your queen and smash this bridge to smithereens!"

"NO!" yelled King Merry bravely. And before the girls could stop him, he charged right into the middle of Firebird Bridge, directly in the path of the enchanted fireworks! The fireworks gathered in front of the bridge, but he stood fast. "I will not let this happen!" he bellowed bravely.

The wizard looked shocked to see
the king. "How…how did you…?" he
blustered. "What are you doing here?"

"I'm here to stop you," King Merry
replied crossly. "You've already ruined
the festival – but you are not going to
ruin this bridge!"

"Oh, yes I am," the wizard replied,
although the girls could see that his

hands were shaking on his crystal ball.
"My queen demands it and I must obey.
So you'd better get off the bridge unless
you want to be blown up too!"

The Storm Sprites emerged from the
tower and flew over to the wizard,
rain drizzling from their thunderclouds
on anyone they passed. "Do it!" they
snapped. "You told Queen Malice you'd
destroy it!"

"She'll be furious if you don't," one added threateningly.

"She'll turn your beard to ice," another laughed.

"She'll put slug jelly in your shoes," the first one cackled. "And make you clean out the stink toad pens!"

The wizard swallowed and looked from the Storm Sprites to King Merry. "I cannot disappoint my queen," he declared. "I will destroy the bridge. Even if the king is standing on it!"

"I can't watch," cried Trixi, covering her face with her hands.

"What can we do?" asked Jasmine. "We've got to get the wizard back into the fairytale book – but how?"

"Maybe we can distract him," Summer said, twisting her blonde hair round in her fingers anxiously.

Ellie glanced across to where the firesmiths had abandoned their fireworks. "We could try setting off the rest of the fireworks," she suggested. "That might distract the wizard for long enough for us to get him back in the book."

"It's worth a try," Jasmine said, running across to the firework area.

"Be careful," Trixi reminded them. "Fireworks are very dangerous. Don't do anything without me."

The girls and Trixi hunted through the firework area. There was a gigantic catapult that had been used to launch some fireworks, and all sorts of crates with exciting labels on them like STARBURSTERS, ZINGERS and SWIRLING SCREAMERS. But when the girls hunted through the crates, they discovered they were all empty.

"Everything's already been used," Ellie said, sifting through piles of ash. "We'll have to think of something else."

"Here's one!" Summer cried, holding up a slim red rocket. "Although the wizard probably won't notice one tiny firework going off if he's about to cause a gigantic explosion."

"Unless…" Jasmine paused. "Trixi, could you use some magic to make this firework even more spectacular?" she wondered.

Trixi nodded. "I'll try," she said, tapping her pixie ring.

"Little red rocket, hear my yell
And stop the wizard casting his spell!"

A spark of light flew out of her pixie ring and lit the end of the firework. "Stand back, everyone!" Trixi cried.

The girls stepped away hurriedly as flames licked up the firework. For a moment Ellie thought nothing was going to happen but then, all of a sudden, the firework shot off into the sky with an enormous whoosh.

CRACK! High up in the air it exploded with golden light.

Jasmine gasped as the sparkles flew into the shape of a beautiful red and gold bird with outstretched wings and a long, sparkling tail.

"It's a phoenix firework," Trixi cheered, clapping her hands together. "Perfect!"

Everyone stared at the phoenix firework in amazement, including the wizard and the king. As they watched, a golden glow spread over it and it began to shimmer and change. With a massive, bright flash, the firework turned into a real phoenix, with golden-red feathers and a flaming tail!

Flight of the Phoenix

All the brownies, elves, mermaids and water nymphs crept out of their hiding places and gasped at the magnificent sight. "Wow," breathed Summer as the phoenix flew overhead, its wings spread and its red-and-gold feathers glistening. "It's amazing!"

The phoenix gave a flick of its fiery tail and began to chase after the wizard's firework beasts. One by one, the beasts burst into harmless sparkles that fizzled away to nothing.

"Hurry up! Destroy the bridge!" the Storm Sprites urged the wizard, but he was staring at the huge phoenix, now heading straight for him.

Suddenly the beautiful phoenix looked menacing as it flew towards the wizard, its powerful claws outstretched.

"Help! Queen Malice, save me!" the wizard wailed, running away so fast that his hat flew off and landed in the river. His crystal ball slipped from his hands and smashed into a million pieces. The girls watched as the shards of crystal turned into glittering dust and blew away.

The phoenix gave chase, swooping down to pick the wizard up in its claws. The wizard dangled in the air helplessly, kicking his legs. "Help!" he cried again.

"He's got him!" Summer cried as the magical bird flew high in the air once more.

"And he's heading our way," Jasmine realised. "Quick, where's the fairytale book?"

Trixi tapped her pixie ring. The book flew out of her pocket, where she'd been keeping it safe, and appeared in Ellie's hands. With another tap, the book returned to its normal size. Ellie flicked through the book to find the wizard's story, her heart pounding. This was their chance!

Once she reached the right page, a dazzling light poured out from the

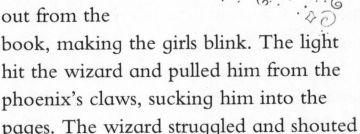

book, making the girls blink. The light hit the wizard and pulled him from the phoenix's claws, sucking him into the pages. The wizard struggled and shouted

but he was powerless
against the magic.
Moments later,
with a last flash
of light, he had
completely
vanished.

"Hooray!"
cried Ellie,
hugging
Jasmine and
Summer.
"We did it!"

"Well done, girls," Trixi laughed,
kissing them each on the nose. "Well
done, phoenix!"

Not everyone was pleased though. One
of the Storm Sprites stamped his foot.
"Pathetic," he muttered.

"Rubbish," one of the others agreed.

At the sound of their voices, the phoenix turned and opened its red-and-gold wings wide. Then it swooped towards them, eyes glittering. The Storm Sprites took one look and fled, hurriedly flapping away into the night.

The phoenix looked as if it was smiling as it flew down to land beside the girls. Summer could hardly believe she was standing next to the beautiful creature.

King Merry's face was full of joy as he bustled over to them. "My dear friend," he called to the phoenix. "I am delighted to see you. May I say how welcome you are back in the kingdom. You have been sorely missed."

The phoenix bowed his head respectfully to the king, then spoke in a rather gravelly voice. "I am happy to have returned," he said. "It is clear to me that a brave and strong leader is ruling the Secret Kingdom again, so my kind can now return. Let the towers be lit once more!"

The brownies and elves began to appear from their hiding places and a gasp of delight went round as the phoenix took flight and swooped up to the first tower, lighting its flame with his fiery tail. As the flames danced brightly on the tower a massive cheer rang out, and Jasmine, Summer and Ellie clapped so hard that their hands tingled.

The phoenix flew the length of the bridge and lit the second tower, and as soon as its flame began to burn, more and more phoenixes appeared in the sky, their fiery tails glowing red and gold.

"This is so beautiful," Summer sighed as the phoenixes made shimmering patterns in the dark sky, swooping and diving together.

"It's better than any firework display," agreed Jasmine. "Hooray for the phoenixes!"

"Let the festival begin!" King Merry declared.

All the people watching cheered and spilled out onto the bridge. Trixi tapped her pixie ring and the lanterns all shone with light again. As the phoenixes flew overhead, everyone began to celebrate.

King Merry didn't seem able to stop grinning. "Thank you, thank you, thank you," he said to the girls, shaking their hands in turn. "Not only did you rescue me from my nasty sister and the wizard, but you managed to send the wizard back into the book *and* bring home the phoenixes too. Bravo!"

"Thank you," Summer said shyly.

"But it wasn't just us," Ellie pointed out. "It was your bravery that brought the phoenixes back to the Secret Kingdom, remember."

King Merry blushed and looked rather pleased. "Well, yes, I suppose it was, wasn't it?"

"It's the perfect way to end the festival," Trixi said, admiring the swooping phoenixes above.

"Absolutely," the king agreed. "From now on, the Phoenix Festival will become an annual holiday for everyone in the Secret Kingdom. You'll have to come back next year, girls!"

"Oh, yes please," Jasmine said at once. "I wouldn't miss it for anything. It's been brilliant. I've never seen such amazing fireworks before."

"Talking of fireworks," Summer said, "I suppose we should go back to our firework display in Honeyvale."

"Yes, of course," Trixi said. "I'd almost forgotten about that."

Ellie gazed up at the phoenixes, feeling a bit sad to be going home. She loved being in the Secret Kingdom so much!

Trixi noticed the expression on her face. "Don't worry," she said kindly. "I know we'll see each other again soon. There are still two fairytale baddies left to find, don't forget."

Ellie nodded. "And we'll make sure they go back into the book with all the others!" she said determinedly.

"That's the spirit!" cried King Merry. "Goodbye, girls. And thanks again!"

Once everyone had said goodbye, Trixi tapped her pixie ring and a sparkling whirlwind appeared, carrying the girls away from the Secret Kingdom and back to Summer's bedroom, where they landed with a soft bump on her bed. Rosa the cat blinked as if she could sense something strange had happened, but then went straight back to sleep, purring.

"That was fun," Jasmine said, putting her earmuffs back on. "Let's go and see some more fireworks now!"

"At least these ones won't attack us!" Ellie joked.

Summer laughed, making sure to turn off the light as they left her bedroom and went downstairs. Then the three girls ran back across the field to find the rest of their families, just as the first fireworks soared up into the sky above Honeyvale Hill.

Bang! Crack! Whoosh! Red, green and blue sparkles burst into circular patterns, and rockets banged. Ellie, Jasmine and Summer linked arms and stood together while they watched the show.

"I love fireworks," Ellie said happily. "Magic ones and real ones."

"Me too," Summer agreed. "And I love our adventures in the Secret Kingdom even more!"

In the next Secret Kingdom
adventure, Ellie, Summer and
Jasmine go to a

Fancy Dress Party

Read on for a sneak peek...

Dance
Disaster

"You're on in a minute, Jasmine,"
Summer Hammond whispered to her
friend.

Jasmine Smith grinned. "Brilliant!" she
said. She was playing Cinderella in the
end-of-term show at school, and this
was the final dress rehearsal. The first
performance was at seven o'clock that

evening and Jasmine could hardly wait.

Their other best friend, Ellie Macdonald, was sitting with the orchestra on the other side of the stage, holding her recorder. "Good luck," she mouthed at Jasmine.

Jasmine waved, then smoothed down her costume. "Do I look okay?" she asked Summer, twirling round. She was wearing a tattered grey dress and a grubby white apron, and her long, dark hair was tied up under a handkerchief.

"You look perfect!" replied Summer. "Those ragged clothes are just right for Cinderella."

"Ready, everyone?" asked Mrs Benson, the girls' teacher. "Here we go." Flicking back her blonde pigtails, Summer picked up the script and opened it at the first page. She'd be prompting in case anyone forgot their lines. Summer was really happy to be behind the scenes with a book, helping her friends – she'd hate to be out on stage performing like Jasmine.

At a signal from Mrs Benson, the orchestra began to play and Jasmine ran onto the stage. Grabbing a broom, she pretended to sweep the floor. "There's so much work to do," she sighed, saying her line clearly so that even people at the back would be able to hear. Then she started her dance.

Summer watched delightedly. Jasmine had been practising the dance for weeks, and she skipped and twirled across the stage happily. Jasmine wanted to be a pop star or an actress when she grew up, and Summer knew it would be the perfect job for her.

Suddenly Jasmine caught her foot on her skirt. She stumbled, dropping the broom with a loud clatter. Then she stopped, in the middle of the stage, and stared down at the floor, breathing hard.

"Keep going," whispered Summer. The orchestra was still playing. Most of the musicians hadn't even noticed what had happened, though Ellie had stopped playing her recorder and was watching Jasmine, looking worried.

Jasmine didn't move.

"Jasmine!" Summer whispered again.

Suddenly Jasmine burst into tears. As Summer ran forward to comfort her, Jasmine hurried off the stage. She charged straight past the orchestra and

out of the hall. Mrs Benson waved
her baton to stop the music and Ellie
hurriedly put down her recorder and
dashed after her friend, her red curls
bouncing. Summer was close behind her.

They found Jasmine in a classroom that
had been turned into a dressing room
for the play. She was slumped in a chair
behind the costume rail, crying...

Read

Fancy Dress Party

to find out what
happens next!

Secret Kingdom

Have you read all the books in Series 3?

Wildflower Wood
ROSIE BANKS

Swan Palace
ROSIE BANKS

Snow Bear Sanctuary
ROSIE BANKS

Phoenix Festival
ROSIE BANKS

Fancy Dress Party
ROSIE BANKS

Jewel Cavern
ROSIE BANKS

Enjoy six sparkling adventures!

Be in on the secret.
Collect them all!

Series 1

When Jasmine, Summer and Ellie discover
the magical land of the Secret Kingdom,
a whole world of adventure awaits!

Secret Kingdom

Bubble Volcano

ROSIE BANKS

Sugarsweet Bakery

ROSIE BANKS

Dream Dale

ROSIE BANKS

Lily Pad Lake

ROSIE BANKS

Midnight Mountain

ROSIE BANKS

Fairytale Forest

ROSIE BANKS

Series 2

Wicked Queen Malice has cast a spell to turn King Merry into a toad! Can the girls find six magic ingredients to save him?

Look out for the next sparkling series!

In Series 4,
meet the magical Animal Keepers of the
Secret Kingdom, who spread fun, friendship,
kindness and bravery throughout the land!

When wicked Queen Malice casts an evil spell
to reverse the Keepers' powers, it's up to Ellie,
Summer and Jasmine to find each animal's
magical charm and reunite them with their
Keeper – before their special values disappear
from the kingdom forever!

Available
February 2014

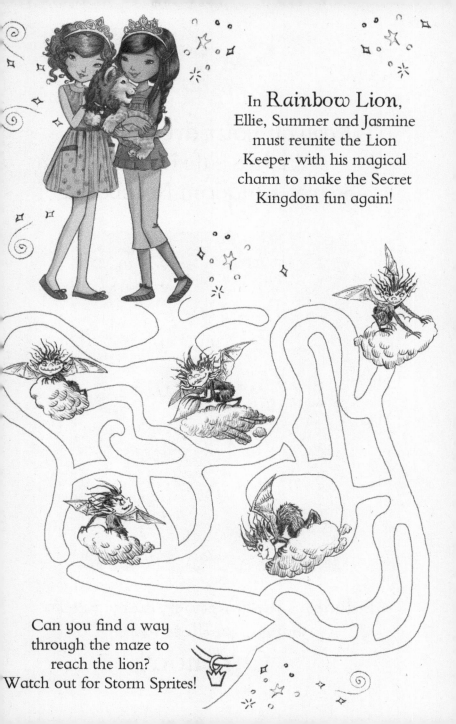

In **Rainbow Lion**, Ellie, Summer and Jasmine must reunite the Lion Keeper with his magical charm to make the Secret Kingdom fun again!

Can you find a way through the maze to reach the lion? Watch out for Storm Sprites!

Keep all your dreams and
wishes safe in the
Secret Kingdom Notebook!

Includes a party planner, diary, dream
journal and lots more!

Out now!

Secret Kingdom

Catch up on the very first
books in the beautiful
Secret Kingdom treasury!

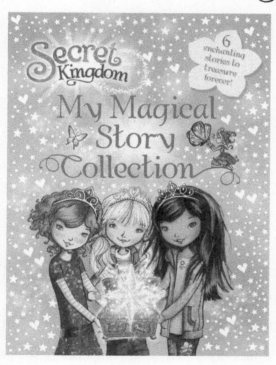

Contains all six adventures from series one,
now with gorgeous colour illustrations!

Out now!

A magical world of friendship and fun!

Join best friends Ellie, Summer and Jasmine at

www.secretkingdombooks.com

and enjoy games, sneak peeks and lots more!

You'll find great activities, competitions, stories
and games, plus a special newsletter for
Secret Kingdom friends!